Published by Grolier Books
© 1996 Disney Enterprises, Inc.
No portion of this book may be reproduced without
the written consent of Disney Enterprises, Inc.
Produced by Bumpy Slide Books
Adapted by Ronald Kidd
Illustrations by Vaccaro and Associates
Designed by Vickey Bolling
Printed in the United States of America
ISBN: 0-7172-8710-6

 **GROLIER
BOOK CLUB EDITION**

I n the city of Paris, the bells of Notre
Dame were ringing. In the street below, a
gypsy puppeteer named Clopin spoke to
the children crowded around his wagon.
"Listen, they are beautiful — no?"
he declared, pointing skyward.

"And high, high up in the dark bell tower lives the mysterious bell ringer. Hush, and Clopin will tell you a tale — a tale of a man . . . and a monster."

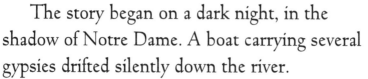

The story began on a dark night, in the shadow of Notre Dame. A boat carrying several gypsies drifted silently down the river.

"Four guilders for safe passage into Paris," the boatman told the group. But as soon as the gypsies stepped ashore, soldiers arrested them!

The fearsome Judge Claude Frollo emerged from the shadows. The judge noticed that the gypsy woman was carrying a bundle. "Stolen goods, no doubt," he said. "Take them from her."

Frightened, the woman started to run. Frollo chased her through the streets of Paris.

The woman ran up the steps of the cathedral
with Frollo galloping after her.

As he grabbed the bundle, she fell and hit her
head. Her eyes fluttered shut, never to open again.

From inside the bundle came the sound of
crying. "A baby?" murmured Frollo. He drew back
the cover and gasped. "A monster!"

The archdeacon of the cathedral told Frollo, "To pay for this woman's death, you must keep the child and raise it as your own."

"Then let him live with you, locked away in the bell tower," Frollo replied. "Someday he might prove useful to me."

Frollo named the child
Quasimodo, which means
"half-formed." As the boy
became a young man, his
form remained as misshapen
as ever. But his strength was
beyond that of ordinary men.
With his strong arms he rang the
bells until they were as much a part
of his life as the stone gargoyles on the
cathedral walls.

When Quasimodo was alone, some of the
gargoyles spoke to him. "Look!" exclaimed Hugo,
peering down into the square. "Today is the
Festival of Fools. Are you going to watch, Quasi?"

Quasimodo just shrugged and went inside.
Laverne watched him sadly and said, "What good
is watching a party if you never get to go?"

The gargoyles followed him into the tower. Quasimodo was gazing at the miniature city he had carved. It was the closest he had ever come to the outside world. "I'd like to go, but I'd never fit in out there," he told his friends.

Victor said, "You should go. It would be an educational experience."

Just then Frollo appeared in the doorway, and
the gargoyles turned back to stone. "Don't even
think about going to the festival," he told his charge.
"They'll laugh at you and call you a monster."

Quasimodo hung his head. "Yes, master," he said.
"You are my only friend."

On the streets below, a handsome
newcomer led his horse, Achilles, through
the crowds. His name was Phoebus. Passing
a gypsy dancer, he stopped and stared. She
was the most beautiful woman he had
ever seen. Esmeralda smiled warmly
at him as she danced
with her goat, Djali.

Suddenly another gypsy sounded a warning. Before the dancers could flee, two soldiers stopped Esmeralda and accused her of stealing.

Djali quickly butted one of the soldiers. As the pair hurried off, Phoebus commanded Achilles to sit on the other soldier!

"Oh, I'm so sorry," Phoebus said. "Naughty horse!"

One of the soldiers
waved his dagger at
Phoebus. "I'll teach
you a lesson . . .
peasant!" he raged.

Phoebus pulled back his cloak, revealing a
captain's uniform. "At ease, Lieutenant," he said.
"And now, would you please direct me to the
Palace of Justice?"

Once at the palace, Phoebus was taken to Frollo. "Well, Captain," the judge greeted him, "you've arrived just in time to help me stamp out the gypsies. We're searching for their hideout, a place they call the Court of Miracles. When we find it, we will crush them like ants."

Frollo didn't know it, but Quasimodo had
decided to join the festival, after all. Caught up in
the wild celebration, Quasimodo stumbled and
landed at the feet of Esmeralda. Quickly he pulled
his hood over his face.

"Are you hurt?" she asked.
"Here, let me see." She drew
back the hood and said, "There.
No harm done. By the way,
that's a great mask."

Later, Esmeralda danced. Quasimodo gazed at her, remembering her kindness.

At the reviewing stand, Frollo and Phoebus also watched the beautiful dancer.

Next it was time for the big event —
choosing the ugliest man and crowning him
the King of Fools. Esmeralda encouraged
Quasimodo to participate, but soon the
crowd realized who he was.

"It's the bell ringer of Notre Dame!" someone
called. At Clopin's urging, the people crowned
Quasimodo as the new King of Fools.

The cheers soon changed to jeers, however, as the people turned against him.

Quasimodo saw Frollo and cried, "Master, please help me!" But Frollo did nothing. He wanted to teach Quasimodo a lesson about disobeying him.

Esmeralda could not stand the cruelty. She freed Quasimodo and faced Judge Frollo. "You mistreat this poor boy the same way you mistreat my people," she told him.

Furious, Frollo cried, "Captain Phoebus, arrest her!" But Esmeralda got away. She disguised herself and slipped into the cathedral with Djali.

Phoebus managed to follow her. Esmeralda faced her pursuer. When she lunged at him, Phoebus said, "You fight almost as well as a man."

"Funny, I was going to say the same thing about you," she replied.

Phoebus promised Esmeralda that he wouldn't arrest her in the cathedral. When Frollo arrived, the captain kept his word. "She claimed sanctuary," he said. "We can't arrest her here."

Frollo turned to the young gypsy woman. "I have soldiers at every door," he said. "Set one foot outside and you'll be arrested."

After Frollo and Phoebus
had gone, Esmeralda took a
moment to pray for all the
world's outcasts. When she
looked up, she saw Quasimodo
watching her. She and Djali
followed him up to the bell
tower.

Esmeralda was amazed
to see Quasimodo's toy
model of the city. Beyond
it were the bells, which he
introduced to her by name,
as if they were people.

"You helped me," Quasimodo told her. "Now I will help you." He gathered Esmeralda and Djali into his arms and swung down the side of the cathedral, out of the soldiers' view. Reaching the ground, he said, "I'll never forget you, Esmeralda."

Then Esmeralda handed him a necklace. She told him if *he* ever needed sanctuary, it would lead him to the Court of Miracles.

When Quasimodo climbed
back up, Phoebus was waiting
for him. Quasimodo growled,
"No soldiers — get out!" He
chased Phoebus down the stairs,
swinging a burning torch.

Phoebus told him, "If you see Esmeralda, tell
her I didn't mean to trap her here. I was only
trying to save her. And tell her she's lucky . . . to
have a friend like you."

When Frollo learned that Esmeralda had escaped, he was enraged. His soldiers searched the city for her. At one home, Frollo questioned the owners, then ordered Phoebus to burn their house.

Phoebus refused. The judge reminded his captain, "You were trained to follow orders."

"Not the orders of a madman," Phoebus replied.

Frollo sentenced Phoebus to death on the
spot. But someone wearing a cloak
and hood was watching from the
back of the crowd.

It was Esmeralda! She picked up a stone and flung
it at Frollo's horse. The animal reared. In the confusion
Phoebus leaped onto Frollo's horse and galloped away.

"Get him!" cried Frollo. The soldiers launched a shower of arrows. One of them hit Phoebus. He tumbled off the horse and into the river. The soldiers watched as he disappeared into the water.

But after they left, Esmeralda dived into the river and rescued Phoebus. He was badly hurt.

Desperate, Esmeralda took Phoebus to the cathedral. "Please hide Phoebus here," she begged Quasimodo. "Promise you won't let him come to any harm!"

Quasimodo promised, and Esmeralda hurried away.

Quasimodo hid Phoebus under a table just before Judge Frollo arrived.

Frollo hissed, "I know you helped that cunning gypsy girl escape! She tricked you. But I know where her hideout is," he lied, "and at dawn I will attack with a thousand men." He whirled around and stormed off.

Phoebus heard everything. In pain, he rose to his feet and asked Quasimodo to help him find the Court of Miracles.

"I can't disobey my master again," Quasimodo told him.

"Aren't you Esmeralda's friend?" the soldier wondered. Then Phoebus staggered off to search for the Court of Miracles on his own.

The gargoyles watched as Quasimodo made his decision. He would help his friend!

Quasimodo caught up with Phoebus and showed him the necklace. "It's a map," he said. Together they followed it to a cemetery. They went down a secret passage, and soon found themselves surrounded by gypsies disguised as skeletons. Clopin accused the two of being Frollo's spies.

"These men aren't spies! They're our friends!" shouted Esmeralda.

The gypsies listened as Phoebus warned them of Frollo's planned attack. "I never could have found you without Quasimodo's help," he added.

"Nor could I!" said the booming voice of Judge Frollo. Without knowing it, Quasimodo and Phoebus had led the judge and his soldiers to the hideout.

Frollo accused Esmeralda of being a witch. She would pay with her life. Phoebus and the gypsies were arrested, and Quasimodo was chained up in the bell tower. Soon it was time for Esmeralda's sentence to be carried out.

"Your day has come, gypsy," Frollo told Esmeralda as he lit the fire.

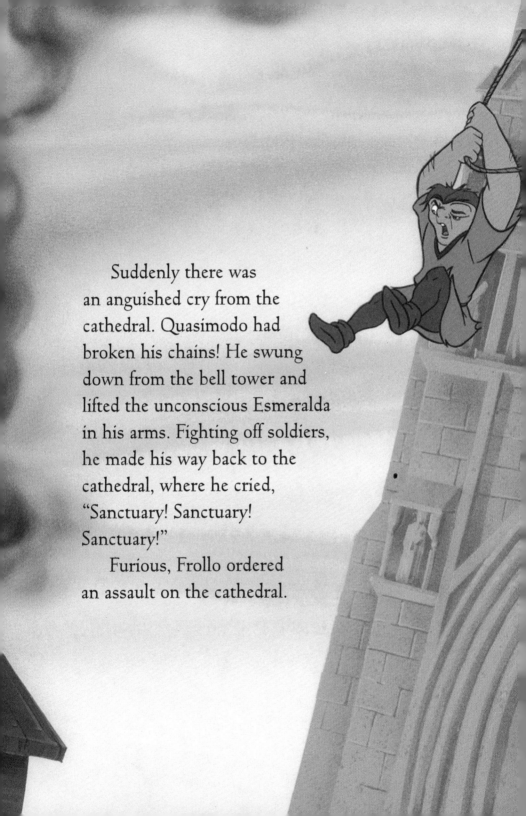

Suddenly there was
an anguished cry from the
cathedral. Quasimodo had
broken his chains! He swung
down from the bell tower and
lifted the unconscious Esmeralda
in his arms. Fighting off soldiers,
he made his way back to the
cathedral, where he cried,
"Sanctuary! Sanctuary!
Sanctuary!"

Furious, Frollo ordered
an assault on the cathedral.

In the confusion, Phoebus escaped. He freed the others and called, "Citizens of Paris, Frollo has declared war on Notre Dame herself. Will we allow it?"

"No!" they roared.

With the help of Hugo and Victor, Quasimodo heated up a vat of molten lead. Just as the soldiers were about to batter down the cathedral doors, he poured it to flow out of the down spouts of the bell tower. The soldiers scattered.

"Come and see, Esmeralda. We've beaten them back!" cried Quasimodo. But Esmeralda did not move.

As Quasimodo kneeled by his friend's side, Frollo appeared in the doorway. Quasimodo saw that Frollo meant to harm him. They struggled, and Quasimodo knocked Frollo to the floor.

There was a soft moan behind them. Esmeralda was alive!

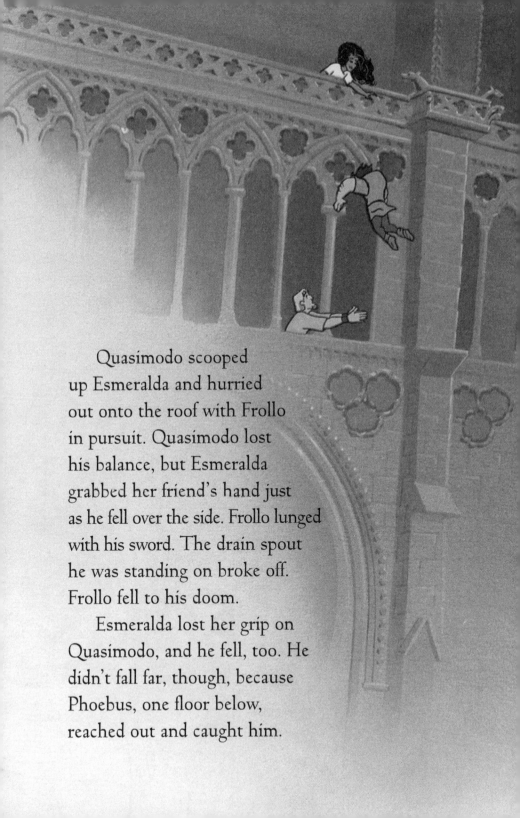

Quasimodo scooped
up Esmeralda and hurried
out onto the roof with Frollo
in pursuit. Quasimodo lost
his balance, but Esmeralda
grabbed her friend's hand just
as he fell over the side. Frollo lunged
with his sword. The drain spout
he was standing on broke off.
Frollo fell to his doom.

   Esmeralda lost her grip on
Quasimodo, and he fell, too. He
didn't fall far, though, because
Phoebus, one floor below,
reached out and caught him.

As dawn arrived, the doors of the cathedral opened. Phoebus and Esmeralda walked into the sunlight hand in hand. Behind them, shy at first and then growing more confident, was Quasimodo.

Cheering, the crowd lifted Quasimodo onto their shoulders and paraded him through the square. Quasimodo, the hunchback of Notre Dame, knew that he was a prisoner no more.